Sealing Her Fate

C.H. James

Golden Storm Publishing

Contents

Sealing Her Fate – Operation: Curves – Book One

Paperback - First Edition

Copyright © C. H. James 2023

All rights reserved.

Cover designed by Golden Storm Publishing

Join the
C.H. James
Community!

STEAMY STORY. HAPPILY EVER AFTER. HOT HEROES.

GIVEAWAYS. FREE BOOKS.
WEEKLY NEW RELEASES.

Make sure you don't miss out on any of my new releases by signing up for my newsletter.
Sign up at chjamesbooks.com NOW!

C.H. James
xoxo

Blurb

To serve and protect. Meet the alpha males who have pledged their allegiance to kick ass. Finding love is a distant distraction to serving their country and saving the world. Until now.

Ryan 'Storm' Brooks
Given leave after a grueling campaign, I return to Falls Creek a scarred man.
I've seen things. Heard things. Felt things.
The noises are always there. It's impossible to switch off. I'm broken.

Except when she's around. Her curvy beauty distracts me from the trauma.
One hot night is all it takes, and I'm falling hard.
That's until the last mission catches up with me. She's there to catch me when I fall, but just because I'm a Navy SEAL doesn't mean I've got the strength to carry on.

The Brooks brothers are home. Four strong, hard, dangerous Navy SEALS have conquered their secret mission, and

only one objective remains: finding love. A return to Falls Creek has these heroes smitten by the curvy women of their dreams. Signed, sealed and delivered, these big guns won't let go once love strikes.

CHAPTER ONE

Ryan

I SWIPE MY AVIATORS from across my brow, allowing the dusty heat of my hometown to kiss my bronzed skin for the first time in over a year.

"Home," I whisper, searching across the landscape where I grew up.

Neat family homes line the streets. Each of them with a perfectly maintained front lawn. Giant towering trees shadow the road splitting the street. Everything is as green as the deep rainforests of Myanmar and a shiver trickles down my spine at the memory of our latest mission.

It's top secret - of course. I couldn't tell you if I wanted to. Being part of the top SEAL team means I'm sworn to secrecy. Divulging any facts of the General's orders would violate the code that I've held my heart and sworn to uphold.

I jumped from a helicopter into a dark world of unknown with my brothers two months ago. They aren't figurative brothers either. No. Not like my 'NAVY Bro's' or anything like that. My family is a proud SEAL unit. All three of my brothers are on *Seal Team Four* alongside me.

The day my youngest brother, Jack 'The Rig' Brooks completed his BUD/S training we knew he was destined to join us at our post, which at the time was deep in the Middle East.

That's what it's like being a SEAL.

I've given my heart to my country.

I've sworn to protect my citizens and my homeland. No matter the cost.

And being on a team with three of my brothers, I'm protecting my own flesh and blood with every mission we're assigned.

A shiny red vehicle slowly drives past, and the window rolls down. A whisper of a breeze cools my cheeks as an arm slides out of the car and waves. I lean down and see my old school friend Nate Jennings gripping the wheel.

"Ryan! Welcome home, mate!"

I tilt my head, allowing a tight smile. "Nate. Thanks." I look over the roof of his flashy sports car to the family home I grew up in. "It's good to be back."

"I'll say! You hanging out in Falls Creek for a while?" Nate's brows shoot up and I notice the Championship Ring on his finger. "It'd be good to catch up. Maybe we can see a game? Those new hockey players are making an impact in the league."

I snigger. I've been cut-off from the world of competitive sport while on assignment, but I've still heard about the bad boys of Falls Creek's new ice hockey team.

"Sounds good to me, man."

Nate flashes a grin. I know he's a football man, but jocks are jocks, right?

"I'd better roll on. Welcome home, Ryan."

The gentle hum of the expensive sports cars exhaust fades down the street. I cross over to open the tall white gate, strolling past the plush green gardens that my mother tended with her own bare hands. Gardening was her passion right before her and dad took of to Hawaii for a well-earned retirement.

"Storm! Oi, STORM!"

My heart races at the sudden yelling. My sensitivity to any sudden movement is still heightened. You try spending two months inside a jungle trying to decipher the difference between a monkey swinging through the trees and a guerrilla terrorist trying to stealth kill you from behind.

A slap on my back forces me to twist on the spot. My boots grip in the grass, but I manage to clench a fistful of the giant figure sneaking up on me and force him back with a hard shove. My heart is racing, and my teeth are clenched so hard they're grinding out a squeaky noise.

"Whoa… Whoa…" Benjamin holds his hands up, his grey eyes pleading innocence. My older brother stumbles back and we're inches away from squashing the blooming lilies. "Relax there, bud. Hold up."

Benjamin finds his feet and pushes back against me. The second my brain focuses on his shaved head, the salt and pepper hair leads my narrowed gaze towards the scar above my older brother's right eye. It's unmistakable. I was there when that fucking asshole gave it to him – I thought he was done for.

"Shit," I breathe, brushing down Benjamin's shirt with shaky hands. "Sorry, man."

"I know we just got back home, but you need to find a way to wind down." Benjamin rolls his arm around me and leads me inside the front door of the house. We all share the family home mom and dad left for us whenever we return to Falls Creek. "It was tough out there. I get it."

Tough? Tough?!

We were on the verge of being held prisoner, but yeah... it was *tough*.

"Here. Have a beer."

Benjamin slides a beer across the counter, and I settle down at the breakfast bar. The familiar smell of home fills my lungs as I force deep breaths in. I remember sitting at this very bench with the man who's pouring a bowl of tortilla protein chips into a bowl. We were kids. Teasing and tormenting each other so much we'd end up rolling on the floor, punching the shit out of each other. Mom would throw a bucket of water over us like we were wild dogs – it was the only way we'd stop laying into each other.

Ben's always been someone I've looked up to. He leads by example. Both at home and on mission. He's a natural leader, and someday, I know he's going to make a damn good father.

"So, you going to catch up with that old flame of yours?" Ben sips his water and looks over the top of his glass to me, clearly trying to help my mind to relax.

"Who? Sarah?" I scoff, shaking my head at the thought of seeing my ex-girlfriend.

"Was that her name?" Benjamin looks away, but I know damn well he knows her name.

I swear when we were dating, Sarah and my brother had better chemistry than I ever had with her. We weren't a good fit.

It's always been that way with the ladies. I've never been in love. I've had girls. Women. It's difficult to maintain a healthy relationship when you're a military man, though. Not to mention the training I pushed myself through to become a SEAL. It takes up so much of your time and before you know it, you're in a gun battle in the dusty backdrop of the Iraqi deserts.

"Yeah. Sarah McBride. She's some sort of event planner or something these days…" I draw on my beer and lift my head to Benjamin. "Where's your beer? What's with the water?"

Ben lifts the glass of water to his lips and winks so the scar above his eye crinkles to a fold. "I'm not putting that shit in my body. We might be on leave, soldier, but your body is still your number one weapon." Benjamin smirks and as he does, he looks over my shoulder and I feel that weird urgency rising in my blood again. "Speaking of weapons, here he is!"

"Boys." Maverick, the other 'middle child' struts up and pulls a stool out beside me. He looks down at my beer and meets me with a confused frown. "Did the Commander give permission for intoxication?"

My eyes pop. "We're on leave, right?"

"Yeah… I dunno, man. Here, hold it up next to your face and smile. I'll send it to the General and ask him what he thinks." Maverick's expression is deadly serious. He grabs my beer and tries to push it against my face while he dives in his pocket for his phone.

"Fuck off!" I growl, forcing the freezing glass of my beer away from my cheek.

"What? Do you want us all to get in shit because you're too much of a greedy fucker that you can't abstain from alcohol the second you arrive home?"

Maverick pins me with a hard look and a gut-wrenching feeling twists in my stomach. He might be the shy brother, but he's got me on edge right now.

"It's… I'm…" I gasp for words and turn to Benjamin, begging him to back me up. He simply holds his hands up like he did a few minutes earlier in the garden. I turn back to Maverick and stare down at the beer.

I'm about to grab the bottle and tip it out when Maverick's mask drops. He slaps me on the back and cackles a tormenting laugh.

"Just fucking with ya, Storm." Maverick beams, his deep voice a different tone to his usual straight edged manner as he exclaims my 'on-duty' nickname. "I'm about to head out for another case. I assume you'll be chipping in to cover the next one if you plan on drinking them all?"

Before I can reply, the youngest of us all bursts into the kitchen with a skip in his step. "Fuckers, fuckers, fuckers! How good is it to be home?"

I guess everyone is more relaxed than I am.

"What's the plan, Jack?" Maverick spins on his chair and greets our younger brother.

Jack's already stopped shaving. His beard is getting thick, and it's only been four days. He knows the second the Commander in charge sees it when we return to California, it'll be stripped off his face quicker than he can say 'terrorist', yet he insists on growing it every time we're given leave.

"There's a movie premiere in town," Jack says.

Benjamin chokes on his water behind me. "A premiere? In Falls Creek?"

"Yeah." Jack nods, holding the olive-green military hat he's wearing. "Apparently some local chick did a lot of the voice over and special effects work, so they've come to town for a one-night special airing."

Maverick and Jack start chatting about the movie. I sip my beer and sink into the chair. I've been set on getting the house to myself for a few hours ever since we arrived home. Judging by the way Benjamin's face is lighting up at the animated description that Jack is giving about the new action film, I might just get that chance tonight.

"So, I've got four tickets. Here…" Jack reaches in his back pocket and passes around tiny white tickets which are stamped '*PREMIERE*'.

I grab mine and look down. *Fuck.*

"Come on." Jack waves over his shoulder. Despite being the youngest, Jack has that leading quality that made him an instant favorite among the platoons. "We'd better get going. It starts soon." My brothers all follow closely behind Jack, and I hesitate. "Ryan! Come on, man. We'll miss the start!"

I clear my throat, clenching the ticket in my fist. "I think I might just hang out here, boys…"

Benjamin's large steps fall silent on the wooden floorboards. Maverick's swaying on the spot and he's stolen my beer without me even noticing, but he's glaring at me like I'm the enemy.

Jack takes a deep breath and retreats to my side. My stomach gives a weird jolt and I know my brothers well enough to know they're not going to just abandon me. Especially not after what happened…

Jack clutches my shoulder, dropping so my eyes meet the deep coffee brown of my youngest brother's eyes.

"We know that last mission was tough on you," Jack says, his voice gentle. "But we're home now."

I gulp down. All three of my siblings are staring at me. Three giant Navy SEALs. Three huge heroes who I admire every single day. I think it's sympathy they're offering, but I can't be sure.

We were all there. They saw what I saw.

No matter what, the Brooks brothers are always side by side. We might be on leave. And technically, right now, we're not a unit.

Except we are.

We always are.

"Fine." I puff my chest out and force a smile. "Fine. I'll come."

Before I know it, we're stumbling out of the Jeep and across the scorching hot pavement towards a bustling crowd gathering at the edge of the theatre on Main Street. Events like this don't come to small towns like Falls Creek very often, and I swear everyone in town is beaming like an excited dog as they approach the red carpet.

"Holy shit!" Jack beams at the head of our group. "This is incredible."

Maverick and Benjamin follow closely behind, but something across the roped off section has me stumbling across to get a better view.

"Fuck..." I breathe, my chest suddenly exploding like a fucking hand grenade has gone off.

A short distance that feels too far away, stands a beautiful woman. Not just any woman. No. She's the most stunning, curvaceous girl I've ever laid eyes on. Long brown hair, wavy like the ocean is drenched with streaks the color of sweet, sticky caramel. My heart skips a beat and I'm gripping the rope distancing me from the flowing dress that's flapping in the gentle breeze.

My body straightens beneath the burning desire to jump the rope and go across to the gorgeous girl, and as it does, she spins and I nearly fall flat on my face.

I swear she looks at me. The honey brown of her eyes lingers, searching and scanning. My muscles tense and my hands curl around the rope, gripping so tight they're shaking.

For a moment, I feel the heat between us, and then it's gone.

CHAPTER TWO

Willow

T HE BUZZ OF THE crowd is building.

They're all here because of me!

I force myself to settle. Brushing my palms down my hips, I feel my dress clinging to every bump and lump of my body. I've spent hours and hours choosing my outfit. Finally settling on a floral dress with a bright white fabric felt like the right choice at the time, but now in the burning sunshine of the red carpet, there's no hiding the sweat patches.

"You'll be fine," Sarah McBride, the local girl who's put this event together, holds my arm and smiles with a reassuring gaze. "You'll pose for a minute. Sign some autographs and then everyone will move inside."

"Autographs?" I'm gasping. I'm just a girl who's done some fancy effects on the newest Hollywood blockbuster. I'm not even *in* the movie. Not really. "Who would want my autograph?"

Sarah giggles and holds the clipboard to her chest. She scans the crowd and points across to a group of school-aged girls who are standing there beaming like Johnny Depp has just walked by.

"Start with them."

Sarah gives me a shove in their direction and before I know it, I'm clutching a Sharpie and signing my autograph. This isn't what I expected when I moved to Falls Creek. This is a small town. A community. Tiny streets with beautiful homes and large, private backyards.

That was the difference between here and Hollywood. I had a chance to hone in on my craft and become the best. Graphic design school had helped, but we're all shaped and molded to what the industry wants. Just like societies expectations of what we should eat, our appearance and what we watch on TV, everything was tailored to suit the commercial world.

I'm different.

I'm a passionate girl who's set on doing things differently.

I've always done things my way. Sure, maybe that's why I've never had a proper boyfriend and my only friend from high school lives in England and is dating some professional footballer in London.

I've questioned everything I stand for and wondered whether I'm making huge mistakes by not falling in line with society.

And then I landed this job.

My unique eye for special effects and graphic design stood out against other applicants. I was the perfect choice for the next mega-hit film set in a future modern world where robots rule and threaten to take over the human race.

Finally, I'm on the red carpet. Perhaps I've made it after all.

"Thank you!" A short girl with curly red hair bounces on her heels as I pass her booklet filled with autographs back. "Oh my god! I can't believe I got your autograph!"

A burst of excitement fills me – my first fan. I smile at the girl and turn my focus to the next young boy, only the red-haired girl reaches across and grabs my forearm.

"Oh, what's your name?"

Like a truck has come and hit me fair in the face, my entire body slumps over. She's not a fan. She's just a girl following everyone else in the crowd. My signature is just a symbol of celebrity to her.

"Willow. Willow Sanders."

The girl runs off and my gaze follows her until she disappears behind a group of four large men. They pull me in instantly, their aura and oozing testosterone make them pop from the crowd like a muscle-soaked nineties boyband.

Holy shit.

It's muscle. Intensity. Rugged handsomeness like I've never witnessed.

All multiplied four times over.

My legs carry me over and I'm standing before the guys, struggling to breathe. A hand slides over my shoulder, and I force my eyes away from the attractive men. Sarah is beaming across the rope at the stack of muscle, too. At least it's not just me who's heart might be bleeding at the sight of these hunks.

"Well, well, well…" Sarah taps her clipboard with her pen. "It looks like we have some special guests tonight, Willow…"

I gulp down.

Yeah, the friggin' A-Team.

"R-really?"

"The Brooks boys are back in town…" Sarah says, moving over to stand directly in front of the guy who's piercing electric blue eyes haven't stopped roaming over my body since

I stepped over. "Hello Maverick… Jack… Benjamin…" Sarah spins and faces the man who won't take his eyes off me. "And Ryan."

Ryan looks at Sarah, but his eyes quickly dart back to me. I'm caught in the middle, and I can't feel my legs. Sarah's tapping her foot, waiting for him to acknowledge her, but he's unmoving. Tension grips the air, and I can feel the frustration boiling over on Sarah's face. I feel like there's a history here somewhere, a previous relationship or bad break up…

Ryan doesn't seem to give a shit.

This man must be nearly seven feet tall. His jaw is chiseled like it's been cut from stone. Short nut-brown hair is neat, but tiny specks of grey make me think he's substantially older than me. There's a seriousness in his expression; a determination that I admire.

Attraction simmers in my belly.

I've never felt this exposed beneath another person's stare.

But he won't look away.

I don't want him to.

Even just standing near these men, I feel protected. Guarded. It's like nothing will ever happen to me again. They're certainly no nineties boyband – no fucking way.

"I guess you're all on the VIP list?" Sarah huffs, running a finger down her clipboard. When she looks up, she tries one last glance at Ryan, but it's no use.

My feet find a mind of their own. I drift across so I'm directly under Ryan's smoldering gaze. I hold my hand out, doing my best to ignore the scent of his cologne which is currently making my ovaries double over.

My wrist is limp and shaking. I never do this. I don't introduce myself to anyone, let alone hunky muscle men.

For whatever reason, this just feels... different. Almost like it's... It's... Meant to be.

To my relief, Ryan's stiff expression softens the closer I get. The intensity of those electric blue eyes doesn't – they're ripping a hole in my chest, hammering directly on my heart.

"H-hi..." I mumble, my hand shaking. "I'm Willow. Special Effects and Sound Engineering."

Suddenly the relentless sun and searing heat is gone. Time is standing still.

A cutting wind blows across my body and the second Ryan reaches out to shake my hand, my dress flies up. There's screams and squeals from other women, and out of desperation not to show the world my fat bubble butt, I yank my hand away to hold my dress down.

Ryan's hand remains outstretched, gripping the air where my hand was moments ago.

"Oh! Damn!" Jack, the youngest looking of the four guys, is bouncing up and down, cupping his mouth with laughter as he jumps on Ryan's shoulders. "She fucking did you in! She got you good, man! Got you good!"

My stomach clenches. *Shit.* I didn't mean to pull away.

It's too late. Ryan is being smothered by his brothers. They're barraging him, laughing and making fun because apparently, I've played a brilliant trick on him.

And now, Sarah is tugging at my arm so I can't do a damned thing to fix it.

"Come on," Sarah hustles, leading me away from those exotic eyes. "It's nearly time."

I can hear the jeers behind me. The brothers are giving it to Ryan like only siblings can. I bite down on my tongue. I want to break free and run back, grab his hand and never let it go.

But what the hell was that?

I've never been in love before. I'm a lone wolf. Always have been.

But that… That was something.

"Sarah…" I hustle alongside Sarah who's racing forward and glancing down at her watch. "Who are those guys?"

"The Brooks brothers?" Sarah frowns at me. "They're in the Navy. Well, Special Forces. Ever heard of a Navy SEAL?"

My chest tightens. "Of course I have."

"Yeah, well… They're all SEALs. Four brothers. They're more famous in this town than you'll ever be."

"Wow…"

"Yep." Sarah pins me on the spot and grips me by the shoulders. Her silky black hair is pulled so tight her brows look permanently surprised. "Listen to me - don't get involved with them. They'll pull you in, promise you the world and their heart…" Sarah's eyes glaze over and that's when I know it for sure – she's got a history with them. "And they'll up and leave the very next day."

Sarah slaps me on the back and when we reach a door leading to the side of the building, she stops me and orders me to wait. The shade of the building cools my skin and there's no one else around. Another violent gush of wind races around the narrow walkway and I'm pushing down on my dress again.

"Stupid dress! Urgh!"

I lean back against the wall and stare down at my hand. It's tingling. Still waiting to glide across the palm of that giant, hunky looking man. My heart is still racing, only now, the words Sarah warned me with are rattling around inside my brain.

That connection was instant.

Those eyes. Those arms. The way his neatly cut hair was receding, showing his years of wisdom.

If I felt it, surely he did, too?

Forget about him.

It's not like a Navy SEAL would ever go for someone like me. I'm the complete opposite of him. I make pretend noises for fictitious plots in movies and low-budget television shows. There's nothing real about that.

He's a real hero - day in, day out. He's literally saving lives and defending my home.

I suck a deep breath and force it down in the depths of my chest. My debut as a sound engineer in a blockbuster film is about to broadcast in the town where I live - I should be excited about that.

Standing tall, I brush my dress down and lift my chin. A rumbling from inside the building rattles the silver steel door, and when I go to step across to peer inside, I'm thrown off course by the sight of a rough looking man, dirty-faced and scowling as he eyeballs me in a way that can only spell trouble.

Panic fills my insides. My stomach sinks. The tall man is skinny. His arms tensed up and his fists clenched. Dirt is smeared across his cheeks and his jeans are torn. My breath is coming out in fast pants. I feel my cheeks heating. No. They're *burning* as he approaches closer and closer.

Suddenly my entire body feels like it's paralyzed. My feet are stuck. I can't move. The scary man is feet away from me, a devilish look in his eye. He rolls his sleeves up and his greedy gaze slides across my body, making me squirm on the spot.

Shit. Shit! SHIT!

I look over my shoulder. I have no idea where I am. I just followed Sarah, lost in conversation about the Brooks brothers.

There's no security around. No one in sight. Fuck.

I clench up, helplessly slamming my eyes shut and waiting for the worst to happen.

With one final gasping breath, the last thing I see before fading into darkness is a body diving across in front of me, tackling the man to the floor.

CHAPTER THREE

Ryan

"**G**ET THE FUCK AWAY from her you piece of shit!"

My wild voice echoes off the walls. The momentum of my jump forces us to roll across the concrete. I make sure I use my strength to straddle the fucker and pin him to the ground. My knee is hard against his jaw and flashbacks of being in the jungle enter my mind.

I strain hard to rid them away. *Not now. Not now.*

"What the hell are you doing man?"

His eyes are wide. Popping with fear.

Good. I hate mother fuckers like this.

"I've been watching you the moment you walked past me, jerk," I growl, curling a fistful of his shirt and using it to shove him hard against the ground. "I could see it in your eyes you sick bastard."

I look down at the bloodshot eyes of the man – and that's when I see it.

No matter where you go in the world, every town has people like Johnny Evans. He was a troublemaker in school. Judging by the way his eyes are sunken and his tiny, bony body feels brittle and fragile beneath my frame, not much has changed.

"Johnny Evans." My nose twitches beneath my snarl. "Trust it to be you."

Johnny looks up at me. His hands are shaking and his lips trembling. Pathetic.

"Please," Johnny begs, whimpering like a lost dog. "Let me go. I wasn't doing anything…"

"Bull shit." I shove him hard in the ground again. "You're telling me you weren't about to-"

"Ryan! Ryan!"

I look up and the door to backstage has flung open. Sarah McBride is racing across. She has a headset and microphone on now. She still looks like the girl I left behind over 10 years ago. There was no connection then, and there's still nothing now.

I give Johnny one final shove and force myself to my feet. I brush down my front but hold my boot firmly on his chest.

My heart is pounding. My lip won't stop twitching. Rage simmers through my veins.

When the smell that sent my stomach into a fuzzy ball of mush moments ago on the red carpet tickles my nostrils again, I force my gaze up and see the stunning honey brown eyes. It's like magic happens right there. Those eyes. They have an instant calming effect over me.

"Th-thank you…" Willow says, her breathing still wild and flustered by the prick beneath my foot. "Security is coming… I don't know what to say…"

Without thinking, my body glides across to Willow and I'm reaching down to grip her hands. I might have missed out on a handshake, but when I pull her hands into mine and hold them, it's so much better.

My muscles tighten the second our hands touch. Her eyes soften and a flicker of something I don't recognize forces me to inch even closer.

It's like the world doesn't exist right now.

Silence.

Warmth.

I'm holding this woman. The electricity between us is sending more adrenaline through my veins than when I'm about to jump from an airplane at 35,000-feet. My stomach is bursting with life. Tiny, excited pops tingle my insides and they're shooting around like a speedboat giving chase.

She's stunning. Gorgeous.

No.

She's so much more than that.

Her beauty from across the distance was enough. But now... Now I'm standing with her hands in mine, barely knowing the woman inside, yet I still know that she's the most incredible person I've ever met.

It's her lips. Begging to be kissed with the plumpness of a sweet, delicate peach. Her cheeks are flushed, red and heated from what's gone down. Only when she offers me a tight smile, petite little dimples pebble her cheeks and my heart aches for her.

"You don't need to say anything, sweetheart," I whisper, my voice raspy. "I'm just glad I followed him... Now you're ok..."

"You... You followed him?"

"Yeah," I nod. "He was acting fishy in the crowd. I didn't realize who it was. If I knew, I would have been on it even quicker. He shouldn't have gotten anywhere near you."

"I've seen him in town a few times… He's not a good sort, is he?"

Willow glances down to Johnny who's been rolled over by security and cuffed. There's a satisfied feeling deep inside of me. They train you to be alert in the Navy. My brothers are on at me endlessly to 'switch off' when we're on leave.

I can't switch off. Not after seeing the things I've seen.

I can identify when something doesn't feel right. It's part of my role to protect these shores, but sadly, sometimes these shores are just as dangerous.

"Urgh…" Sarah steps up and clears her throat. Her green eyes are popping at Willow and I as we stand there hand in hand. "I'd hate to break this up… But Willow… We're starting any minute now. Are you ok to go on?"

Willow nods at Sarah and then looks down at our hands. *She doesn't want to let go either.* Sarah taps her foot, but when I give her a hard look, she knows me well enough to know to back off.

"You know what's weird?" Willow says, taking the tiniest step forward so her chest presses against me. "This doesn't feel weird."

She grips my hands harder. She squeezes.

And my heart damn near explodes.

"No. No, I guess it doesn't."

A lump forms in my throat.

She's left me once already tonight. I can't let Willow leave my sight again. Who's knows what will happen if I'm not around to protect her. It sounds crazy, but everything inside of my soul is screaming out at me to make sure this woman is protected every minute of every day.

And I'm going to make damn sure I'm the man to fulfil that duty.

"Come on," Willow squeaks, her dress flapping around as she spins and clasps my hand down beside her hip. She doesn't let go – she'll never let go again. "You're sitting with me for the premiere."

Before I can tell her how much I would love that, Sarah is on our case, shaking her head.

"No, no, no, no, no… No!" Sarah barks, barricading the door.

Behind us, Johnny is groaning as the security guards drag him away. Willow clenches my hand firmly and steps forward, looking over Sarah's shoulder into the theatre. It's packed out. The entire town of Falls Creek is waiting for the premiere to begin, excited chatter filters through the doorway Sarah is blocking.

"The seating plan is already laid out." Sarah points to the clipboard she's been holding like it's made of fucking gold.

"Who's sitting next to me?" Willow asks, leaning on her tiptoes to see the floorplan.

"Well… Me…" Sarah hums, her eyes darting around.

I watch as Willow's dreamy honey eyes twinkle. "You'll have to give your seat up for the man who potentially saved the evening then, won't you? If it wasn't for him, the show would be over. You can't introduce the star of the show if she's out in the alleyway being mugged, or God knows what else by a crazy man…"

Willow smiles and her entire body straightens like a proud lioness. Sarah's eyes flick between us and a flashback of the girl who I dated briefly after high school enters my mind.

Sarah's intense. She's always been full on. But she's still a good girl with a big heart.

And dammit, if she let's me sit next to this bombshell, I'll damn near drag my brother to her place so they can go ahead and start hitting it off like they threatened to all those years ago.

"Fine." Sarah rolls her eyes. "But hurry up. They're waiting to introduce you."

Willow bounces and shoves Sarah to the side without another word.

The theatre is dark, and I follow in behind Willow, gripping her hand tighter than ever. There's an announcement before the start of the movie, and when Willow stands in front of the entire audience and waves, accepting her applause for the role she's played in Hollywood's latest action movie, I smile like a chum in the front row.

Grinning from ear to ear, I cross my arms and watch the woman who's rocked my entire world within a matter of hours. I feel pride in the same way I do when my team completes a mission. My heart races when I look at her. The second she returns to her seat, I reach out and collect her hand, returning it right where it belongs – in mine.

After being gripped to the edge of my seat for the length of the movie, I rise to my feet alongside a few hundred Falls Creek locals and applaud the end credits. Willow twirls around and holds a hand up, accepting the admiration of her work before the theatre slowly thins out as people move towards the exit.

"Wow," I say, grinning down at Willow who's swinging her hands in front of her body like a shy girl. "That was amazing! How did you get that laser beam effect in that final scene?"

Willow smiles. "It's just a combination of layers upon layers of graphics… All moving in sequence…"

She could be saying anything right now, but all I care about is the way her lips move as she talks. Glossy. Red. Juicy. My mouth fills with saliva and I've never wanted to kiss anyone so badly. Willow continues talking, guiding a strand of caramel-streaked hair behind her ear as she sways on the spot.

She's the sweetest thing I've ever laid eyes on.

I nod my head and step in closer. Pretending to listen when really there's only one thing on my mind. Willow notices the heat searing between our bodies but continues talking until I press my finger against her lips, gently lowering it down as she falls silent.

My heart pounds inside my chest. Slowly, I lean down and press my lips against hers.

An explosion detonates inside of my body. It's a hot rush of tongue and lips all at once. Willow wraps her arms around my neck, locking me in and I'm hunched over, smothering her mouth with deep, hard lashes of my tongue against hers.

"Oh," Willow groans, pulling hard against my neck to force me firmly on her mouth. "Don't stop. Don't stop."

I pull away, only for a moment long enough to say, "Never. I will never stop."

CHAPTER FOUR

Willow

STRONG. DEMANDING. *AMAZING.*

Ryan's large hands cup my cheeks. We're fumbling around each other's mouths in a tongue-thrusting kiss.

Luckily most of the theatre has rolled out already. We're alone.

"My God," Ryan groans, arching his neck back to take in my eyes. "You are incredible, you know that?"

He drops his lips back on mine and my mouth splits, permitting further invasion of his tongue against mine. A groan leaves the back of my throat. My hands find a mind of their own, moving down his ridged abdomen to grip his perfectly firm ass.

A tug of my hair makes me yelp with a burst of pleasure. Ryan's handling me in a way that I've been handled. And I like it.

This giant hulk of a man is everything I didn't know I needed in my life.

I'm standing in his arms, and despite the way he's owning my body... The way he's devouring my mouth, gripping my hair and squeezing my wide ass all at the same time...

It's… It's… *Fuck.*

My hands press against Ryan's chest, and we break for a breath. A simmering wave of heat racing across the skin on my arm causes the hairs to stand when I look deep into his dazzling blue eyes. I draw my bottom lip between my teeth, savoring every last drop of his saliva on me.

"Willow…" Ryan breathes, cupping my cheek. "I know we've only just met…" My heart is pounding inside my chest. I can barely stand. "This connection between us. I… I… I just can't…"

It's odd seeing such a brawny bear-like man lost for words. He oozes confidence. His body is the symbol of strength and protection. But even for me, the words to fathom what the spark between us is - it's unexplainable.

"It's ok," I smile and lean up on my toes, pecking the round of his chin ever so softly. "We don't need words. We don't need a reason."

Ryan gulps down so his Adam's Apple effectively bounces. My hands runs down his cheek, the prickly stubble making my core shiver with excitement.

I see the look in his eye. He's scared. Maybe he's just like me – he's never been in love before. And that's what this is. I'm calling it here and now. Hell, I would have called it the moment I caught sight of him. It's seems like too much too soon. And it is.

So why does it feel like love?

I was a sniper propped up in the distance on a hill. I lined my target up and took aim.

Look at me getting all military already.

It's the *Ryan Effect.*

"Sweetheart," Ryan steps back, rolling his hands over me so his forearms rest on my shoulders. He lowers down and those electric eyes draw me in. "I'm going to buy you dinner."

"I'd love that."

"Good. And after that, we'll have dessert. And coffee."

"Ok. Anything you want."

Ryan's voice vibrates against my chest. I'm standing in his arms, feeling safer than I've ever felt.

"After coffee, I'll take you for a walk and we'll see the sun set."

I nod, grinning. He's planned it all out for us. I'm his mission and he's moving in. I've never felt more wanted. He won't take no for an answer. And I won't give it to him.

This is one target that he's not going to miss.

****

Ryan never lets go of my hand as we walk in the diner on Main Street – *The Creeky Diner.* The howling wind that bothered the patrons at the premiere has finally died down, and the evening sun is warm enough to keep comfortable in my dress and heels.

"After you, my sweet," Ryan says, holding the door for me and bowing slightly as I slide inside the diner before him.

"Such a gentlemen," I smirk. "Are you going to pull my chair out for me, too?"

I'm joking, of course. But when we move over to the table, Ryan's already holding the chair at a twisted angle, allowing my behind to slide in the gap and settle down opposite him. I'm wondering if this man can get any more perfect.

"So," I chime, lifting the menu up. "You were raised here, right?"

"Born and bred. Falls Creek through and through."

"So you know what the best thing on the menu is then?"

Ryan chuckles and his addictive warm smile teases my body. "It's been taken over since I was last here. But knowing the Stewart family as I do, I would recommend the tacos. Mama Stewart is one hell of a cook and an even better lady."

My heart skips a beat. He's so passionate. So full of life and enthusiasm. He's everything I've needed in my life for so long.

"Tacos it is."

"I'll have the same," Ryan smiles. He reaches across and grabs my menu, rising from his seat and grabbing a bottle of water and pouring me a glass. "I'll go and order. You stay here and relax, ok, my sweet?"

My sweet.

"Thank you."

Ryan spins and I can't help but watch his sweet, perfectly shaped ass as he trots across to order at the counter. He's wearing tight chino pants, cream-colored and the cuffs rolled up. The button up shirt he wore to the premiere is untucked and ruffled at the bottom.

I stare across the busy dining room. I'm smiling like a goofball, watching Ryan as he shifts his weight from one leg to the other while ordering. His plump, firm ass is making me warm inside and all I want to do is lay him on this table and bite down on those sweet cheeks. That's my dessert. Right there.

"Shouldn't be too long." Ryan settles back down opposite me, his giant body bumping the table as he rests his forearms on the edge. "So what's next for you after the premiere?"

I shake my head, trying my best to stop thinking about the muscles staring across the table at me.

"Well, I have a few smaller projects to tidy up," I say. "After that… Who knows…"

Ryan smiles and his eyes turn to slits. He leans back and folds his arms across his chest. "I admire that, you know?"

"What?" I frown.

"You don't have a plan. You're happy to just let life take hold and you'll see what happens when it comes up," Ryan proclaims admirably. The blue in his eyes brightens for a moment before he takes a sip of his water.

"I guess… It's scary, too." Ryan raises his brows and I hear it. "I know. It's not your kind of 'scary'. I'm not exactly fighting a war like you."

A waitress appears from the kitchen, two steaming plates making their way over to us. She drops them down and I smile up at the girl who looks about my age.

"Two tacos and a side-" She stops and stares at Ryan. "Ryan? Ryan Brooks?"

She jumps up and down, clapping her hands together. Ryan's eyes pop open and he's smiling weakly. My heart beats hard against my chest and I can't help the painful thump that's making my stomach wrench.

"You're back in town?" The brunette girl with a body shape similar to mine says. She's still bouncing on her heels as she drops the bowl of guacamole to the table with a clumsy crash. "Is Jack back, too?"

Ryan shuffles in his seat. "Yeah. We're all on leave for a few days. Jack's around somewhere."

The girl squeaks. "Yay!"

"I'll let him know you're looking for him, how does that sound, Riley?" Ryan smiles, a cheeky twinkle in his eye that makes me feel more at ease.

"Oh, wow…" The waitress glances over her shoulder to the kitchen where a bell chimes. Her eyes burst with urgency. "Thank you. Thank you. Thank you. Oh, I can't believe you're all back. Welcome home, Ry-Ry."

She spins away and I raise my brows to Ryan. "Ry-Ry?"

"Shut up." Ryan growls playfully. "My younger brother's old friend, Riley Stewart. Her parents bought this diner and she's obviously picked up a job."

I smile and watch the girl grab the plates from the counter. "You and your brothers are like celebrities in this town, huh?"

Ryan shrugs and helps himself to a taco. "I guess so. We don't see it that way though."

"Of course you don't," I chime. "Who knows where we'd be without the help of the Defence Force though, right?"

Ryan doesn't offer a response. His hands rush to find the next taco and he's biting down hard, crunching the hard shell so his mouth is filled. I watch his eyes dart around the diner, looking anywhere except at me.

"Where are you off to after your leave then?"

Ryan looks over his taco at me and gulps down. "Can't say."

"Oh! Top secret, hey?"

"Mmmm hmmmm."

I observe Ryan who collects another taco. He's downed three in the time I've taken two bites. But I don't think it's because he's hungry. No. He doesn't like talking about his job. One mention of the military and he's a closed shop.

Maybe it's because he's not allowed to talk about it. Or maybe there's more to it than that.

Whatever it is, we'll get through it. For now, I'm just happy to be sitting opposite the man who has a thick layer of guacamole above his top lip and corn chips crumbled in a heap on his empty plate.

I giggle and reach across the table, swiping a thumb over Ryan's lip, collecting the green dip. The biggest smile I've ever seen spreads across his features, brightening his eyes so they wrinkle at the edges. His cheeks lift and when I slide my thumb across to his mouth, without hesitation, he sucks hard, sliding his tongue around the knuckle.

My body trembles.

Another twist of his tongue has me melting. Our eyes connect and that smoldering, sexy look is back. Heat flows down my spine, sinking deep in my panties as Ryan's mouth slides off my thumb and ends with a hard suck that pops.

The air surrounding us is suddenly thick. I gulp down and drop my taco.

My hands are shaking.

I need this man. Right now.

"Should we…" My voice comes around croaky, and I clear my throat. "Should we go for a walk or something?"

Ryan smiles and rises to his feet. He steps around - slow and purposefully. From behind, he grips the chair and slides me out. Looking down, his face is hard when he holds an arm out to guide me to my feet.

"Allow me."

CHAPTER FIVE

Ryan

I HOLD MY ARM firm, allowing Willow to lean on me as she steps down the wooden steps leading to the walkway by the river. Even the tiniest touch this woman applies to my body has me burning with desire.

Her perfume is intoxicating. I'm terrible at distinguishing smells. All I know is it's sweet and it makes my fucking heart melt.

It was enough sitting across the table from her. It was too much staring at her as she talked so passionately about her work after the premiere.

And now, we're walking hand in hand as the sun sets over the river. The distant orange hue skips across the gently flowing water. Small ripples in the gentle flow of the river dance to the edges. The bright colors of the setting sun kiss Willow's cheeks and light up her entire face.

She looks beautiful.

"I can't believe I've never walked down here before," Willow sings, her voice as sweet as a drop of candy

I observe her taking in the large oaks trees that line the path. Her beautiful honey brown eyes scan the pebbled stone, and I hold her close; just in case her high heels give way on the soft ground. We watch a squirrel in the distance run up a tree. We laugh loudly as he puffs his cheeks out with his midnight snack tucked away for safe keeping.

"They're so freaking adorable, don't you think?"

I stare at Willow. *You're adorable.*

"Yeah, yeah, they are cute…"

Willow doesn't stop talking. She's non-stop chitchat. And *I love it.*

It's all in the way she waves her hands around as she talks. Her body is a prop for her stories. Her face is a hundred different masks and a variety of expressions that match every emotion that she conveys with her life adventures.

I've only known Willow for a little over five hours, but I'm falling. I'm falling fucking fast.

A breeze blows across the river and the evening air is cooling down quickly. Willow tucks in beneath my arm and her warmth prickles my skin. The second the sun sets in the horizon, we'll freeze. The vivid blue sky has faded, the orange color of the sunset is quickly changing the further we walk.

Darkness is looming but I don't want this evening to ever end.

"How about we sit down here and watch the sun disappear, my sweet?"

I settle down on a bank beside the path. A giant tree trunk acts as a back rest and I guide Willow down beside me, pulling her tightly so she's resting against my chest. I thread my fingers through hers and with the other hand, Willow settles in and runs it down the inside of my thigh.

"This is magical," Willow breathes.

Fuck.

It's all I can do to squint and try to stop my throbbing cock from firming up. Her hot hand is sliding up and down my thigh, teasing me the further up she goes.

Is she doing it on purpose? If she goes any higher, she'll just about cup my balls.

Fuck.

"Yeah, it's one of my favorite spots in Falls Creek," I say, biting down on my lip, stemming the flow of blood to my aching dick.

"Do you think… when you're finished in the Navy, that you'll settle down here?"

Another slide of the hand. "Urgh… Yeah, maybe. I guess I haven't thought that far ahead yet."

Willow twists and when she looks at me, her eyes are wide. "You mean you haven't got *everything* planned out?"

I chuckle and with every bounce my chest makes when I laugh, Willow's hand inches ever closer.

"Not everything. It's tough to plan things out when you don't know if you'll be home-"

I stop myself. *Shit.* I try my hardest not to think like that. My brothers are on at me all the time. '*We'll always make it home, bro…*'

But it's who I am. I've always feared the worst. A pessimist.

"Why wouldn't you make it home?" Willow asks, and I'm instantly regretting everything.

"Oh, that's not what I meant," I lie, gulping down. "Look, the suns almost disappeared!"

I point to the horizon and feel Willow's hand clamp down on my inner thigh. The sinking feeling that had started to build again dissipates beneath her touch.

She makes everything better. I forget about the missions. The gunshots. The wounds. The *dead bodies.*

"Thank you for bringing me here."

Willow's body twists and she slides up and pecks my cheek with the softest kiss. I smile and tuck the only stray strand of her caramel brown hair behind her ear. My hand lingers at the back of her head, we're lost in each other's gaze.

The hardness in my pants is pressing against my zipper. I'm not sure I can hold it back much longer.

My cock throbs and my hand works it's way around to Willow's lips. I pull her bottom lip down, allow it to slide from my thumb. Her plumpness isn't only for those delicious lips. Her every curve is right there in front of me.

The white floral dress is the only thing hiding away her stunning curves. Her cleavage is bursting out, begging to be touched and kissed. Her smooth legs are rubbing against mine as we lay beneath the tree. They're thick, tanned and lead the way to a pleasure center that I intend to occupy as my own territory. I've been admiring her sweet, wide ass all day. Every chance I've had, my eyes would imagine how it looks beneath her dress. How I want to bite it. Smack it and watch it wobble. I want to hold it while I drive deep inside her and plant her with my seed.

I want this woman. I want her more than I've ever wanted anything before in my life.

"Willow…" My hand cups her cheek and I move so my nose glides against hers. "When that sun is set over the horizon, this doesn't need to be over. The night's young…" Willow's eyes darken. She inhales sharply. "Willow, I want to spend the night with you. The day might be done, but I'm not."

I look out to the river and the slightest round of the fading sun is almost beyond view.

Willow shuffles up and her hand lands on my chest. Her tongue swipes across her lips and we're silent for a moment. She stares into my eyes. Into my soul. The leaves rustle above us - the squirrels are doing their final dash. Tiny waves of water break the silence as they lap gently against the riverbank.

Willow leans in.

Without hesitation, I latch on to her mouth and reel her in.

CHAPTER SIX

Willow

"FUCK," I BREATHE, DRAWING a harsh breath before smothering Ryan again.

My hands find the button of his shirt. I rip and something pops across the grass. It doesn't matter. Nothing matters.

All that matters right now is that I have Ryan. All of him. His heart. His strength. His body.

I want it all.

And I want it right now.

I swing a leg over Ryan and straddle against his crotch. My lungs are desperate for oxygen, but I'm not letting him go. My mouth covers his and our tongues are battling against each other. He's hot and wet, his lips tasting sweet and sexy as my hands find the firmness of his bare chest.

"Baby…" Ryan groans through his teeth.

I bite down on his lip and suck hard. His hands work their way around my back, sliding to my hips and squeezing. He owns my body. He owns it like unguarded territory.

I'm not self-conscious around Ryan. He makes me feel like the most gorgeous woman on the planet. The way he's guiding my hips so they grind against the hardness in his crotch. His palms are hot and wild against my body, searching and roaming over every inch of my skin in a frenzied rush.

"I want you now," I moan, my neck rolling back as Ryan's face dives between my breasts.

This dress has been a burden all day, flying up in the wind at the worst of times. Now, it's in the way of his rough stubble prickling against my stiff nipples. Ryan's hands leave my hips, but only to dive beneath my dress and slide my panties down my ass cheeks.

I lean up on my knees, my breath coming out in short, sharp bursts. Ryan guides my panties down and as he does, I'm reaching for his belt buckle. I undo it in a flash, and the second I feel my panties slide to my ankles I'm diving inside Ryan's underwear and yanking his hardness out for some fresh air.

"My sweet," Ryan groans, his firm length gripped in my hand.

I start stroking him. Long, long strokes. He's big. So big. It's the most perfect erection I've ever seen. The engorged flesh is lined with veins, powerful masculinity protruding from several well-rounded inches.

I massage the hot, smooth column of flesh between my fingers. Circular motions take in every inch of him and his groans tell me I'm doing it just right.

"Oh, your touch feels so good. Stroke my cock, sweetheart... Stroke it good."

Ryan leans back on the tree and raises one arm so it flattens the hair on his head. I take a quick scan of our surroundings, guiding my hand up his shaft as I do. We've walked a long way from the diner, lost in each other before settling down to watch the sunset. The sky is almost dark. The tiniest amount of light allows me to see the glowing bulb of Ryan's cock looking up at me.

It's begging to be tasted.

I shuffle down on my knees and swipe a hot tongue over my lips. I'm starving. Parched. All of the above. I just want his hardness of his arousal in my mouth and his come soaking my throat.

Ryan's free hand fists my hair and he's guiding me to his cock. His chest is pounding, I can feel the blood racing through his body and his cock is pulsating. My hand strokes down, pulling him so the drips of pre-cum glisten.

I take him in my mouth. He's fucking perfect. It's hot and silky. It's soft and veiny. Bumpy against my tongue as I slide my mouth down as far as I can.

Ryan moans and when I look up with his perfect cock in my mouth, his eyes are closed and his mouth ajar. He's moaning loudly, unabashed about anything that might be happening around us. Screw the public space. He doesn't care, so hell, I don't either.

His shirt is ruffled from where I've searched for the hot skin of his bare chest. This man is fucking sexy.

A brunt of muscle. A hardened hero. He's my defense. My rock. *My everything.*

I whip his cock from my mouth just to admire him. He's laid back against the tree, his cock rising high in the air like a fucking flagpole. I stroke him fast, curling my palm around the bulb of his end, rotating a sweet massage that has him squirming in the grass with pleasure.

His chiseled features look even more handsome in the dark shadows of the night. The electric blue of his eyes would cut through even the darkest sky.

I stroke his cock and lean down again. My mouth wants more. It will never be enough, but I push my ass in the air and open my throat, diving down as far as I can on his throbbing length.

"Oh, fuck…" Ryan moans, his deep voice vibrating down his body. "Fuck you take it good, baby…"

My pussy is soaked. Ryan isn't the only one aching for more. My core is pulsing, begging to be touched and when I reach down and circle my clit, I see Ryan peek through hooded eyes. His hips begin to thrust. The large tip of his cock chokes me. He forces me to take him deeper. I cup his balls and I feel his cock tensing inside my mouth.

I rub my clit, slapping it with an open palm every time Ryan pushes deeper down my throat. He thrusts and I moan as best as I can with a neck choked with hard male heat. *Oh God*. I want more of him down my throat. More. More. More.

His fist grips my hair – playing with myself while sucking his cock is turning him on. His ass isn't even touching the grass anymore he's thrusting so hard.

A heated ball is building in my belly, and I feel Ryan tensing up inside my mouth. He's going to come. And I want it. I want to taste him.

I lean back and start stroking Ryan. His giant dick is wet with my saliva, and I stroke harder and faster, our eyes staying connected the entire time. My breathing is stuttered, and I shift forward to use my other hand on Ryan's cock.

"Yes, oh, it's coming baby…"

Ryan leans up on his elbows. I'm two hands stroking the full length of him. Pulling, jerking, kneading his enormous arousal. I'm desperate to taste him. Ryan's hands fumble around, and he finds his way beneath my dress. A thick finger slides inside me and Ryan's face turns bright red.

"Fuuuuuuuck!"

I lower down, smothering his dick with my mouth and using one hand to milk his hotness for my own selfish thirst. Hot ropes of pleasure shoot against the back of my throat and he's covering my mouth with his seed. His finger leaves my pussy, instead reaching to grip the back of my head with two hard, firm fistfuls of my hair.

I'm his, all his.

He yanks my hair, his entire body shaking beneath his climax.

I swallow hard. Savoring every last drop before I finally hollow my cheeks and slide off his dick. My tongue swipes and licks, taking every last drop with me.

Ryan shuffles forward and presses a hard kiss to my mouth.

"You're incredible, you know that?" He says, breathless.

I nod, still enjoying the lasting taste of this hunky Navy SEAL. Ryan looks past me and sees my panties on the grass. He looks at me, a wicked smile tracing towards his eyes.

"I want to take you somewhere more comfortable," Ryan says, his handsomeness illuminating the night. "You deserve the best, my sweet. And trust me, this tree isn't a good leaning post."

I giggle and wipe at my lips. "We'd better go now then."

CHAPTER SEVEN

Ryan

YAN

M Y CHEST FEELS LIKE some fucking terrorist has planted a grenade directly over my heart. It's a ticking bomb, ready to explode.

Except it feels right. It's dangerous - yes.

But it's also the most exciting thing I've ever felt in my life.

Willow is everything. One day is what's it's taken to… Taken to…

Fuck.

You know what? To hell with it.

I'm in love with this girl. I'm in love with her!

One day? That's too soon to be able to tell, right? You can't fall in love with someone in one day? You know what… Who gives a fuck! When you know, you know.

I grab Willow's hand and lead her through the gardens. The solar lights have ignited. They light the way towards the front door of my house. My heart is racing and all I want to do is get Willow upstairs.

We battle through the luscious foliage of the jungle. *Shit*. No. It's not the jungle. Garden - we're in the garden.

Willow is breathless behind me – we've hurried home in a flash. Lucky for us, Falls Creek is only a small town and the brisk walk from the river only take a few minutes.

Branches block path and I push through the way forward. The garden is overgrown, and we will need to tend to it before we return from leave. I force my forearm out, pushing the hanging branches aside. The pathway is gravel and it's crunching beneath my boots. *Mom's taken good care of this garden.* I hear a helicopter pass overhead. My head begins to feel hazy, but I can hear Willow's heels clobbering up the path behind me. I push past more trees and wild plants. I hear Willow panting and my body feels just as tired as her breath sounds.

Then, I turn around, it's not her that I see.

It's not Willow holding my hand. The helicopter above me is getting louder. It's right above us. My ears sting and then there are gunshots. Bang. There's screaming. Bang. Bang.

"What the fuck!" I yell. My body sways and I'm yanking my hand from the man gripping me so fucking tight I swear my fingers are about to burst from my hand. "Get the fuck away from me!"

My eyes strain in the darkness. *Where the hell is Willow?* My head spins. I'm searching for my girl. Where is she? *They've got her. They've taken her!* My balance is all over the place. The earth is moving, shaking. Bang. Bang. Bang.

"Ryan? RYYYYAAAN!"

WHACK.

****

"He just needs a rest... It happens every time we come home..."

Benjamin's voice is the first thing I hear when I wake up. My eyes open slowly and I'm staring up at two familiar faces.

"Oh, hello there..."

My heart melts as Willow slides her hand over my chest. She threads her fingers through mine. She's hovering over me, and it takes me a second to find my bearings.

The light shining brightly in my eyes forces me to sit upright. Despite the gasps and over-the-top attentiveness of both my older brother and Willow, I shuffle back against the headrest of my bed.

"What the hell happened?" I ask, scanning the room.

A tray with soaked white washcloths is set on my drawers. There's a cup filled to the brim with ice cubes and a small bowl with three white capsules laying inside.

"We think you've just had... You've had another episode." Benjamin hesitates, and I see him gulp down. "You're tired, bro. Perhaps you should have stayed at home today. We're all sorry for making you come out."

I shake my head and grip Willow's hand. "No fucking way. If I didn't come out today, I wouldn't have met Willow."

Willow swipes at her eyes and it's only then that I see how red and puffy they are. "Yes, but you wouldn't have fainted in the front garden either. This is all my fault... I'm so sorry."

Willow sinks to her knees and she's gasping for breath against my chest. Benjamin offers a weak smile. This isn't Willow's fault; we both know it. It's happened before and I shouldn't have been so stupid to push myself so much. I know this shit happens when I'm tired.

I scrunch her hair in my hand. My chest feels like it's on fire. This isn't Willow's fault. She's not in my head. She doesn't see the things I see. She doesn't know the trauma of seeing the things I've seen.

None of this is her fault. None of it.

"Baby… Baby…" I guide her chin so those stunning honey brown eyes are looking up at me. "This isn't your fault. It probably would have happened regardless. It happens whenever I'm run down and exhausted. It's not the first time. I swear to God, baby."

Willow sniffs and wipes at her eyes. They're so swollen I want to kick myself. I hate seeing my girl like this, especially when I'm the cause of her pain.

"Then we get you the help you need," Willow protests fiercely.

Benjamin slides up beside the bed and his giant frame shadows the light over my face. "Ryan has the help he needs back in California. The platoon offer support and he's not forced to return to duty if he doesn't want to. He's looked after, right bro?"

I nod. "It's not as bad as it used to be."

Willow manages a tight smile. Slowly, she shuffles across and lowers down so her lips press on mine. It's soft at first, then emotion takes over and she clutches both my cheeks and smothers me.

I hear Benjamin to make a weird grunt and when Willow pulls away, he's disappeared from my bedroom.

"I'm sorry if I scared you, my sweet," I say when Willow finally settles on the bed beside me.

"Don't be sorry. I just wish I could have recognized it. I didn't know what the hell was happening. Your eyes disappeared. They glazed over. It's like you weren't on this planet anymore."

"I wasn't. Not really, anyway."

Willow draws in a long, deep breath. Her face is flushed and red. She looks tired – exhausted. When she lets go of the deep breath, I know there's something else behind the massive sigh.

"I'm here for you. No matter what. You know that, right?" Her eyes sharpen on me. I nod and grip Willow's hand. "Maybe we just stay inside of a night? Is that when it's at it's worst?"

"It can strike anytime. It just takes a trigger." I feel my hand ball in the sheets of my bed. I should be making love to Willow right now, not laying here like some sick hospital patient. "I guess the darkness of the night sky and Mom's fucking over-grown garden set me off. My brain took me back to the jungle."

"Do you want to tell me what happened there? You know… While you were on duty? Would that help?"

A stirring feeling rumbles deep in my stomach. I look deep in the eyes of the woman I've fallen so deeply in love with. I've just frightened the shit out of her. We barely know each other, even if it does feel like we've known each other our entire lives.

No one has ever looked at me the way Willow is right now. She's hovering at the edge of my bed like some kind of angel. She's been sent from Heaven to show me that love exists. She's showing me that there is more to life than how I'm feeling when I return home from duty.

I can't trouble her with the details of what happens beyond these shores.

"Willow…"

I clutch her hands and do my best to shove the nauseous feeling in my belly from rising up. Her brown locks slide over her shoulder as she looks down at me, smiling timidly. The simmering in my belly has nothing to do with my PTSD this time. Nope. My body is a nervous wreck because I'm about to say something I've never said to another human being before.

But it feels right. And if my training has taught me anything - it's to go with your instincts.

"Willow… I… I love you."

There's a silence. A long silence.

Fuck. It's a *really* long silence. Or is this just how it is when you put your heart on the line?

Willow's face slowly lifts and her hand clenches mine. She squeezes tight. So fucking tight and before I know it, her mouth is crashing on mine.

"I love you, too. I do, I really, really, really do!" Willow exclaims, her eyes bursting. "Oh God… I thought I was being fucking ridiculous. I mean, can you be in love with someone you just met?"

I grin. "Like you said earlier, we don't have to put words on what this is. But it sure as hell feels like love if you ask me," I grin like a lunatic. Willow smiles and leans down for another kiss. "And listen, I'm sorry I ruined our *plans* for tonight. I promise I'll make it up to you."

"Damn right you will." A deep voice that isn't Willows beams from the doorway and when I look over, Maverick and Jack are both flashing beaming smiles into my bedroom. They steam over and acknowledge Willow before sinking down on the bed either side of me. "Can you at least wait until we're out of the room, though, bro?"

"Oh, Jesus…" I grunt, gathering my balance. "Would you lumps get off the fucking bed? You're caving it in."

"Good to see you're feeling better, brother." Jack's grinning like a child and sipping his bottle of water.

"You scared us, man." Maverick gives my thigh a whack with a soft fist. "You doing ok?"

I nod, taking in the three people who all have that sympathetic frown written across their eyes.

"I'm fine, boys. Hey Jack," I say, attempting to take the focus off me as quickly as possible. "Do you remember that girl Riley?"

Jack puffs out his cheeks and his eyes light up. "Riley Stewart? Are you kidding?" He runs his hands down the air as if Riley is standing in front of him and he's sliding them down her body. "Curves for days. Man, I fucked that one up. Friend-zoned."

Maverick chuckles and shakes his head. Jack's always had a thing for his best friend. We all know it. But clearly Riley, the waitress from the diner, and my brother have trouble showing their true feelings.

"Well, she seemed pretty excited that you are back in town," I say, winking. "Perhaps time away has worked in your favor?"

Jack's eyes goggle and he's reaches for his phone. Without another word, he's racing from my bed with his phone pressed against his ear and bursts from my bedroom.

Maverick and Willow laugh alongside me.

"Well, rest up, Storm. We've only got a few days of leave and then we're back to California. You'll be able to get some sessions in when we get back there to help you, alright, bro?"

I smile and Maverick waves goodbye to Willow.

She settles back down beside me, only this time, she lays down and snuggles into my neck. Gently, she kisses my cheek and trails her fingertips through my hair.

I know I've fucked tonight up. But I'm going to get better. I can only continue to work through this and with Willow's support, I know I can be a better man.

Soon, I'll be the man that she deserves.

"How about we reschedule?" I pipe up, holding Willow's fingers up as they thread through mine. "I'm here for another five days, then I need to return to California."

"Five days, huh?" Willow twists her mouth. "Five days *might* be enough to make it up."

I roll over and pin Willow to the bed, smothering her sweet laugh with my mouth.

"Well how about I start right now?"

"Let's rest for tonight, baby." Willow smiles gently then slowly works her mouth so it's tickling my earlobe. "Tomorrow, I'm all yours, Commander."

CHAPTER EIGHT

Willow

T HE HARDEST THING I'VE ever done was leave Ryan's bedside last night. There was no point in staying there. Ryan insisted he was fine, and he practically begged me to stay with him.

But I figured he would get more rest if I wasn't there talking to him all night.

He needs to get better. He needs sleep.

I stumble into my kitchen and pour a cup of steaming coffee. Glancing out the window, I slurp loudly and grip the mug, absorbing the heat into my cold hands. My front lawn has mildew covering it. A thick fog blankets the street, and it looks like a typical day in Falls Creek – once the fog clears, the day will be perfect.

It won't be perfect without him.

With a deep sigh, I spin around and head for the shower. I let the hot water race down my body and think about the meal at the diner with Ryan. It was perfect. Of course it was. Everything about Ryan is perfect.

I can see his handsome features as the bubbly soap glides over my body. His ripping blue eyes. His shapely jaw, ridged and hard, exactly like him. Those biceps and solid forearms... The way they bulge even without tensing.

My thumb drags across my nipple, and I picture the alluring lips and expert touch of his tongue rolling over mine.

My hand slides between my legs and I pant short breaths.

"Oh, Ryan…"

I moan beneath my touch. My drenched body is on fire, the image of Ryan's hands searching my body spurring me to circle my clit, rubbing hard and sending my knees weak. I'm moaning, a frenzied heat boiling in my core. I rub harder, my tongue swiping my lips, desperate to taste him again.

KNOCK. KNOCK.

My eyes shoot wide.

BANG. BANG. BANG.

"Hello? Willow? Are you home?"

A deep voice zips down the hallway. I slam the tap off and grab my towel, quickly wrapping it around my body.

"Give me a minute!"

My skin feels flushed and hot from the shower, and now I'm sweating new droplets of moisture even though I'm swiping a towel over my body. A deep thumping footstep rattles the front porch, and I can hear heavy boots pacing up and down the veranda.

I yank my dressing gown over me, my body still half wet, and slide out of the bathroom. I find my way to the front door as I attempt to dry my ass crack and rip the door open.

"Oh, good morning!"

Dazzling blue eyes flicker at me and melt my heart instantly. They glow as the morning sun peaks through the thick fog. Ryan's dressed in a tee-shirt and jeans – much more casual than

I saw yesterday. My moistness throbs at the very sight of him, still not satisfied after my shower fun was cut short.

"Ryan…" I choke, pulling my dressing gown tight. My pussy tenses. "Wh-what are you doing here?"

He steps in and wraps an arm around my back, stooping me down and smothering a deep kiss to my hungry mouth. His tongue slides inside my mouth, gliding smoothly with a scintillating, brash kiss.

Ryan pulls away and guides me back up. He lifts a brow and is entire face brightens.

"I missed you last night," Ryan says.

"I missed you, too," I say. "I thought you were resting today? I didn't expect to see you…"

Ryan flaps a hand and turns to face the street. He holds his arms out, his mouth lifting to a wide grin. Closing his eyes, he sucks in two long, deep breaths through his nostrils and exhales loudly.

"It's a beautiful day!" Ryan shouts out, his voice echoing in the streets as he turns to face me. "We only have a few days together. Why waste one cooped up in bed all day?"

A frown pulls my brows. "Um… Because you fainted last night, and you need to look after-"

Ryan lunges forward, his eyes bursting. "Exactly! Now, I've had a good sleep. The best sleep I've had in months…" He reaches down and grabs my hands. "And I think it's because of you."

My stomach drops. Ryan's pinning me with a look I've never seen before. It's admiration. Desire. *Love.* He's on top of the world, and apparently, it's all because of… Me?

"I- I don't know what to say…"

"You don't need to say anything," Ryan says, lowering his hands around my waist. "Let's spend the day together. I can still relax. Spa treatments. Lunch by the river. Fishing."

"It does sound pretty good…"

Ryan presses a gentle kiss to my lips and as he does his hands lower down to the curve of my ass. Our lips lock and it's an instant blast of passion. My breath catches in my throat, the heat of Ryan's body pressing against mine as my mouth opens wide, allowing his tongue to return to its rightful place.

"My sweet girl… Oh, God I missed you…"

Ryan draws my lip in his mouth, biting sucking and devouring me. His hands pull me closer and work their way around the front of my gown, pulling at the tie to loosen it. My heart races.

"We should go inside…" I breathe, reaching behind for the door.

Ryan's eyes flash. "Tell me you're naked under there."

The door creaks as I open it and I poke my tongue between my teeth and tease with a mystical nod. Ryan sweeps his eyes over my body, probing and searching. A growl leaves his throat, like a wild beast entering my home, ready to claim me as his own.

We fumble our way towards my bedroom. I'm leading the way, stepping backwards as Ryan relieves my gown of duty. My naked body crashes on the bed and I don't even care that my plus size, lumpy and wobbly body is exposed.

Blood touches every nerve in my body. Ryan saunters in front of me, tearing his tee-shirt off and tossing it across the room.

A flush scorches my cheeks. It sears through my body and soaks my pussy at the sight of the bulky hero before my eyes.

The body. The muscles. The sexy fucking bronzed skin.

"Holy shit…" I moan, my hands working their way across the bed.

My head is lost in the ridged abs of Ryan's eight-pack. That's right. Eight well defined muscles are crying out to be licked. His pecs are glistening, and I can feel the hours, days, *years* of hard work he's put into his body.

Suddenly my throat is aching.

I lean forward, sliding my hands over the hardness of Ryan's chest. His nipples are hard and slowly I work my way down to his jeans and unlatch the button. I try to guide them down, only to be stopped by Ryan's hand gripping my chin.

"It's your turn, remember?"

Ryan's eyes turn dark. Just like they did last night under the tree. He's a wild beast ready for action and he grabs me by the ankles and pulls my legs from beneath me, tossing me backwards so I crash on the mattress.

The round curves of his bulky shoulders meet my gaze as he crawls up the bed, his hot tongue swiping across his lip. He stoops down and draws a nipple in his mouth. He sucks hard and does the same to my other breast.

"These tits are fucking incredible…"

My eyes are slits as I nod up at him. Ryan slaps my rounded bust playfully, lowering to draw them in his mouth again. Teasing my rosy buds with a gentle nibble, he shuffles his jeans down and I see that he's not wearing underwear.

"Commander or commando?"

I giggle and Ryan's eyes light up. He doesn't offer a word, instead a teasing smile fades as he sinks down my body and positions himself between my legs.

"Spread your legs for me," Ryan says, his hands sliding between me thick thighs. "I want to see your beautiful pussy."

I obey his command. I'd obey anything this man says.

My body is on fire and when my legs part, I feel the moisture between my folds separate. There's another growl between my legs, and when I push up on my elbows the feeling of Ryan's hot tongue lapping at the edge of my moistness sends me crashing back down.

"Oh, fuck!"

I grip the sheets of the bed. He kisses the warm folds between my legs, gliding his hands along the sensitive skin of my inner thigh. He slowly dips his tongue inside me, forcing my chest to gasp for breath.

"You taste better than I thought you would…" Ryan groans, the vibrations of his deep voice tickling my clit.

"Don't stop…"

I push the back of Ryan's head and his mouth smothers my pussy. It trembles and tightens with every kiss. My hips find a life of their own and I'm grinding my core against his rough stubble while holding the back of Ryan's head. My clit feels like it's on fire when I push against his tongue, sliding my entire opening up and down the handsome features of his face.

"Fuck baby… You want to fuck my face, huh?"

I nod, my eyes hooded. Ryan grins a devilish grin and jumps on the bed beside me, quickly lifting me so my leg swings over his face and I'm sinking down over him. We're top to tail - my ass in Ryan's face as that same growl rumbles from his mouth.

"OH! YES!"

I thrust my hips over Ryan's face. I reach out, my hand gripping the long, hard cock that's staring me in the eye. Ryan's tongue fucks my pussy, sliding in and out smoothly as he slaps my ass with a hard hand. Over and over until it stings my cheek raw.

I lower down and take his length in my mouth, twisting my tongue over the red-hot tip of his cock. My hips are bouncing on his face, my head returning to savor every last taste of his magnificent arousal.

My heart begins to beat rapidly. The thudding of my chest working its way down my body, breaking through and scorching my insides as it goes. Every muscle in my body feels like it's contracting and I'm on the edge of exploding.

"Oh, I'm gonna come!"

"Come on my face, baby… Come on me! Come on me!"

Ryan's hand smacks my ass again and I scream out. My hand jerks his hard cock and I'm rubbing my tits with my other hand. He spanks me again. I'm screaming. An uncontrollable fire escapes my belly and races down, rushing through my core and escaping with a burst of liquid squirting all over Ryan's hungry mouth.

"OHHHHHHHH!!!!!"

My hand clenches my nipple. The other Ryan's firm cock.

My hips jerk. My body jerks. My entire fucking world jerks.

I'm shaking and desire escapes my body as I crash down on the bed beside Ryan.

I'm breathless, staring up as Ryan's face appears above me. He wipes his mouth, a teasing tongue licking my moisture from his lips. He's gripping his hardness and his eyes are blazing into me.

"It's time to make up for last night…"

"I... I... I think..." My chest is pounding, I'm struggling to breathe. "I think you might... have... just done that."

"We're just getting started, my sweet."

CHAPTER NINE

Ryan

MY COCK IS ACHING. Throbbing. Pulsating.

There was no way I wasn't coming over to Willow's place first thing this morning. The moment she left my bedside last night, I missed her.

I've barely slept a wink. One hour. Maybe two. And even that was dozing off, only to wake when my head dropped after falling asleep staring at my phone.

But Willow doesn't need to know that.

If I told her I hadn't slept, she'd have me back home. Tucked up and she'd leave again.

Willow needs to know that my heart has been aching for her all night. She needs to know that she means more to me than people I've known my entire life. In a matter of two days, she's become everything to me.

I want to heal. I want to get better. This disorder that's affecting my life needs to be taken care of.

And I'll do it.

But overriding all of that, right now, before I return to base, I want to make love to this amazing woman.

"Are you ready for me, baby?"

Willow's sweet brown eyes look up at me, half-hooded and eager. She's never looked fucking sexier.

"Please fuck me," Willow says, her voice sounding more and more like an angel.

I reach out and guide her legs open. I shuffle forward and notch my cock so it's inches from her entrance.

"You're fucking dripping for me," I growl, staring down at the moisture flowing from the sweet, smooth folds of my beautiful woman. "You like me making you wet, baby?"

Willow bites down on her lip, nodding seductively. She's reaching for her tits, and she rubs them like the good fucking girl she is. Her foot lifts up and she guides it so it slides over my cock. A wicked spike of pleasure hits me. Her knees bend and the second foot comes over and she's got a talent I wasn't aware of - she's jerking me with her feet.

"Woah…" I moan, unaware something so odd could be so fucking sexy. "You're full of surprises."

Willow's feet are warm against my shaft, and she circles her enormous tits while jerking me. My stomach feels like it's on fire and I reach out to slide a thick finger between her folds, dipping in her wetness just so I can taste her again.

I swipe my finger over my tongue, tasting the sweet, tangy cream of my sexy, curvy goddess.

I taste her on my tongue. I don't know if she knows it yet, but now I've tasted her, she's mine forever. I'm never letting her go. From the moment our eyes connected, I felt an overwhelming notion to protect her. To ensure she's safe at all costs.

And I know with the way concern gripped her eyes last night, she'd do the damn same for me. This is more than sex. This isn't just some fling.

This is love. This is real. And this is forever.

"I need you. Now."

I'm done waiting. I want to be inside Willow.

I shuffle forward and loop my arms around Willow's gorgeous thick legs. This woman is perfect. She's round. She's got a bust to be proud of. And her hips… Oh fuck, don't get me started on those hips.

"Ready?" I ask, eyeballing Willow's hungry gaze.

"Please…"

Something inside of me comes alive at the sound of Willow begging me to fuck her. I nudge the tip between her folds and instantly she's moaning. I slide inside, only slightly.

"Fuck…"

It's warm against my knob. Willow's rubbing her tits, twisting her nipples and moaning loudly. The sweet smell of the bedroom is filling my chest and I guide myself further in.

"You're so fucking tight," I grunt, lowering down so my fists are clenched either side of Willow's face.

I smother her with a kiss and push deeper, deeper. The wetness of her pussy heats my entire body and I begin to thrust. Willow hips move with me. She won't stop rubbing herself. I sink down her chest, drawing a nipple and biting down.

"Oh!"

Willow gasps for breath and I push up to pound her harder. Her body is opening for me and when I guide my hand to cup her cheek, Willow moves my hand down around her throat. Her fingers press against mine so I'm applying pressure to her neck. I feel her pussy tighten around my cock.

"You want me to choke you, my sweet?" I gulp down, nervousness gripping my stomach. Willow nods and I can't believe this woman. "Are you sure?"

"Yes… Please…" Willow moans. "I want it. Fuck me hard and choke me, please, baby…"

I suck a harsh breath and give my fingers a squeeze. I've never done anything like it before, but Willow's moaning against the palm of my hand and the harder I squeeze, the more her wetness contracts around my throbbing length.

My hips drive deeper into Willow. My hand clenches around the hollow of her neck and she's growing redder in the face. I release my tight hold, but Willow glares up at me, demanding more.

"Fuck!" I clench my teeth and return the pressure.

I push my entire length inside. I'm up to my balls inside her and I've never felt more alive. Her moisture tightens around me and I'm using her neck as leverage to pound faster and faster.

"Oh!"

Willow chokes a scream and my pace is increasing. A deeper heat fills my body, and I can feel my pleasure desperate to escape. Willow's eyes are popping and her hands clasp around mine, guiding my fingers harder around her neck as we both approach a deeply sensational climax.

"Fuck! You take it so fucking good! Fuck! Yes! Fuck!"

My hips slap against the hot inner thigh and thrashing her soft flesh. My teeth clench together. My lips stiffen and I'm rock hard, ready to explode and plant this woman with my seed.

"FUUUUUCK!"

I scream out, my hand clasping Willow's neck as her body releases her orgasm simultaneous to mine. Her hips ride it out, grinding deep against me so my cock fills her completely. My gripped hand releases the curve of her neck and Willow's breathing through her orgasm as shoots of hot come layer her velvety insides.

The entire room shakes as my body erupts and I collapse down on the bed, struggling for breath.

A few minutes pass and Willow finally rolls over and looks me in the eye. The cheeky, adventurous woman who is going to completely change the way I look at sex is staring at me as if she's ready to go again.

"Best. Sex. Ever." Willow presses a kiss to my chest and rests her head there.

"You certainly had some… different moves…" I chime, smiling.

"A woman needs to know what gets her over the edge, right?"

A flutter ripples through my stomach. "I love you, Willow."

"I love you, too." Willow sneaks up and kisses my lips. "This isn't exactly relaxing, is it?"

I look down at our naked bodies and raise my brows. "I dunno… I feel pretty relaxed."

I feel my eyes suddenly feel heavy. Willow nestles against my chest again, her fingertips circling my skin. I fade into a distant doze, my heart beating against Willow's cheek. The day is just beginning outside, but I'm with Willow.

And that's all that matters.

Now, with her in my arms, I can rest.

I can sleep.

I've found my girl. And she's right beside me, right where she belongs.

CHAPTER TEN

Willow

I LEAN AGAINST THE door frame.

So sweet.

Ryan's chest rises and falls. He keeps making this cute snorting noise that makes me giggle every time he twitches. For such a giant of a man, he looks so innocent when he's sleeping.

Gentle and tame.

I slide the door closed and move out to the kitchen. I grab my phone and slide to check my messages. They haven't stopped rolling in today.

The premiere has been a great success right across the country. The movie is a hit in Hollywood and the special effects and sound engineering are being applauded in all the right circles. My phone blew up right after I snuck away from Ryan, so I've been letting him catch up on some sleep.

My agent is swamped with offers, and when my phone starts vibrating in my hand, I swipe to answer the call.

"Hello?"

"Willow! Congratulations!"

My heart jumps at the excitement in my agent's voice. "Thank you, Gabby!"

"Sweetheart, I can't keep up with the emails. You're in demand, ma girl!"

A squeak leaves the back of my throat. This is what I've worked so damned hard for. This is why I've moved to Falls Creek. I've really knuckled down and perfected my craft. I stand out now, and the rewards are about to be reaped.

"That's amazing. Thank you so much."

"I'll start sending some offers through, but sweetheart, your next move needs to be the right one. This is your chance to start climbing that wobbly rope, girl. Get to the top and stay there."

Gabby's voice rings out and when she hangs up, I drop my phone to the bench.

"What was all that about?"

A deep voice filters from behind me. I twirl around and the beaming smile of Ryan is striking me in the heart.

"Oh, hey! I didn't hear you get up…" I tread over and link my hands over the rounds of Ryan's bare shoulders. "How are you feeling, my tired little baby?"

Ryan grins. He has some dried drool in the corner of his mouth, and an imprint of the pillow is still creased in the rough unshaved stubble on his cheek.

"I feel good…" Ryan leans down and presses a kiss to my lips. "Who was that on the phone?"

"Oh, just my agent…" I flap a hand, doing my best to be nonchalant.

"Oh yeah… It sounded like good news…"

I lead Ryan across to the sofa and we settle down. The excitement filling my belly is nearly bursting out. It's the first time I've ever had someone who I've genuinely wanted to share my good news with. And Ryan's only adding to that because his eyes are illuminated and eagerly waiting for me.

"So, the movie is going down really well…" I start and Ryan's gripping my hands so tight they might burst. "And my agent is flooded with new job offers."

Ryan beams and starts bouncing on the sofa. "That's amazing! Well done, babe!"

Ryan's giant arms embrace me warmly. I can't wipe the smile from my face.

I've got it all. Within two days, I've achieved more than I have since I left college. I've found an amazing, supportive man who I'm comfortable around and I can be true to myself. I don't have to fake who I am around Ryan. I don't have to pretend to be someone I'm not.

And my career looks set to blossom. All my hard work has paid off.

"So what does all this mean?" Ryan asks, chewing his bottom lip.

"I guess I just sift through the offers and go from there…"

There's a gush of wind outside that pushes against the window, causing it to creak. Ryan twists on the sofa and there's a vein pulsing in his neck. He gulps down, focusing outside where the vicious wind continues to blow.

It's late afternoon; Ryan has slept for most of the day. The sun will be setting soon, drawing a close to another day. It's another day gone that I should have spent with Ryan.

Instead, it's been wasted.

Except it's not a waste.

Nothing to do with Ryan is a waste.

I look across at my strong protector. He's off in the distance, staring at the leaves lacing the door leading to the backyard. I can feel his mind ticking over, sorting the information and processing it. It's what he does – assess the situation and make a plan.

"Ryan…" I lean in and draw his eyes to mine. "What exactly is this…" I wave a finger between Ryan's bare chest and myself. "Us. You know…"

Another gulp. *Fuck.* My chest feels like is going to explode.

Ryan clears his throat. His brows shoot up. "Argh… Um…"

His eyes draw in on mine. The vivid blue dives deep inside of me, pulling me closer and closer until I'm latched to his bottom lip. I kiss him, hard, passionate and rough. Our tongues swirl and it's a steamy mess.

"Baby…" I moan through another swipe of his tongue. "Baby, I don't want you to go."

Ryan bites down on my lip, his hands working over my body as he leans back, breathless. "Stay here. Stay in Falls Creek." Ryan's voice is desperate. "We'll settle down here. Have a family. You can still work, right? You can still live your dream from here?"

I nod, tears threatening in the corners of my eyes. "Of course I can. So long as I have a computer, I can work anywhere for the right contract."

Ryan's entire face brightens. "Then let's do it. Willow, I love you. I have one more year on active duty, then I return to these shores. I'll be home and we can work the rest out later."

I jump to my feet and pull Ryan up with me. He wraps his arms around me and lifts me up. My legs leave the ground and he swings, holding me and never, ever letting me go.

"I love you so much, Ryan. Our life is going to be perfect together."

"I love you, too, my sweet."

****

As soon as we set foot back in the Brooks household, Ryan's brothers swarmed us and insisted we join them for dinner at the diner. After a quick ride in the Jeep, I'm tucked up beside Ryan, his arm draped over my shoulder in a booth as Jack and Maverick stare across at us.

"What I don't understand…" Jack pulls his sunglasses from over his eyes. "Is how Ryan can get a lovely lady in two days, yet, I can't even get a girl to have a drink with me…"

Benjamin, the eldest of the brother's towers over the table with two glasses of cola gripped in his hands. His expression is hard as he stares down at Jack and shakes his head.

"Perhaps that's because you haven't showered in two weeks…"

Jack scoffs. "Fuck off. Asshole."

Ryan chuckles beside me and I grip his thigh underneath the table. He leans over and sneaks a kiss.

"I've just gotta go to the bathroom," I chime and rise to my feet.

I straighten my top out and shuffle across, turning to see Ryan watching my ass the entire length of the diner. I reach the door to the ladies bathroom and wink back at my boyfriend, pushing forward and quickly doing my business.

After I finish washing my hands, a familiar face emerges from the cubical beside mine.

"Oh, hello, Sarah!"

The silky black hair of the girl who organized the premiere looks much tamer today. She's wearing a free-flowing sundress and her green eyes match the emerald green tiles of the bathroom.

"Hey Willow! What are you doing here?"

"Oh, dinner with Ryan and his brothers."

Sarah's brows waggle and her plump cheeks blow out. "Oh, wow! I saw you and Ryan yesterday." She flaps a hand over her face like she's flushed. "Hawt, babe! Hawt!"

We share a laugh and walk out of the bathroom together. Sarah is excited to hear about all the job offers flying in. As a hard working girl herself, she congratulates me on my efforts to get where I am.

"Well, I'd better get back to my table." I look across and Ryan's staring across the room, clearly awaiting my return because he's tapping the seat I've deserted beside him. "It's nice seeing you."

Sarah waves and by the time I'm settled back beside Ryan, she's out the door.

Ryan's hand quickly returns to my thigh. I sip my cola and feel the hard glare of Benjamin Brooks searing into my cheek.

"Um, what?" I ask, frowning.

Benjamin's scowl is harsh. His nostrils are almost flaring across the table at me, like some kind of raging bull. I feel exposed… Targeted. But he's not directing it at me… Is he?

I move under Ryan's arm and he cuddles me in close. Everything feels safer when I'm within touching distance of Ryan Brooks. He's my protector.

"Sarah McBride," Benjamin growls fiercely. "What's her deal?"

I shrug, looking across to the door where Sarah just left. "Her deal? Like…" My eyes light up. "Wait. Are you interested in her?"

Benjamin's face remains stiff. "I can't divulge such information."

I glance at Ryan. Then to Maverick. They're too busy studying the menu to see the look in Benjamin's eye. It's intense. Dark and bold.

"Oooooo…" Jack gives Benjamin a playful shove and the mask appears to break. There's an exchange of push and shove between the two brothers and when I catch Jack eyes he leans across the table, dodges an opened-palm slap across the face and says, "He always gets like this when he falls *in love…*"

"Fuck off! Asshole!"

Benjamin smacks Jack across the head, and just as the play-fight threatens to break out on the floor of the diner, the sweet waitress from the other day comes across and stands above the table.

"Now.. Now…" Riley Stewart says, tucking a strand of her auburn hair behind her ear. She looks Jack up and down and he's instantly straight-backed and still. "Jack Brooks. You haven't changed."

Jack gulps down. "Riley. H-how are you?"

Ryan giggles beside me. His chest bounces as we watch Jack rise to his feet, hold his hand to his forehead and salute Riley like she's his Commanding Officer.

"Please tell me I wasn't like that when we met…" Ryan whispers in my ear and I shake my head.

"Oh no. Jumping a crazy man in an alleyway is a bit different to a salute." I giggle and slide into Ryan's arms. "Mind you, you might still have a way to go in the bedroom… You might be good at getting the girl… But keeping her satisfied?"

Ryan's mouth drops. "Take that back. You haven't seen anything yet."

"I hope not, *big boy.*"

Ryan grips me and pulls me in a playful hug. He's become everything to me. And I know even when he leaves in a few days time, he'll return.

He'll come back for me, and I'll damn well wait for him.

My hero. My Commander.

My love.

EPILOGUE

Ryan

ONE YEAR LATER

"Right about here, I think…"

The shade of the tall tree is the perfect spot, so I throw the blanket down and roll it out. Willow sets the picnic basket to the side. I make sure she doesn't start taking everything out.

She can't see inside.

"It's further away from the diner than I remember." Willow looks back up the path. "You really must have had me smitten. I walked all this way in heels, remember?"

I chuckle and a smile meets my lips at the memory of our first night together. "We even walked home after…" Willow snaps her neck around and smiles at me. "Well, we both know what happened down here."

I start emptying the contents of the picnic basket and when I find the tiny black box, I subtly shove it in my pocket and open the champagne.

"To one entire month together!"

Willow hods her glass out as I pop the cork and it flies off into the river. It's the perfect afternoon – and it's about to get even more perfect.

"I can't believe they're letting you take four weeks off," Willow says, sipping the bubbles. "You must have impressed on that last mission. Are you sure we're not going to get sick of each other by the end of this? We've never spent this much time together…"

My brows furrow. "You mean you're taking time off, too?"

"Well, yeah," Willows shrugs.

"So because you're some sought after graphic designer you can just do as you please now…"

I smile and poke my tongue out. Willow just shrugs and says, "Pretty much, yeah."

I tilt my glass up and tap it against her. "Well fucking cheers to that, babe."

Willow settles down, resting her back against the tree. It's the same tree we used as a bedhead after our first date. I still remember it like it was yesterday. It was the day my entire life changed.

I've been back on mission with my three brothers. We continue to uphold the highest of standards expected of a Navy SEAL. My disorder is under control more than ever, and the doctors back in California think it has a lot to do with the fact that I have something else to occupy my mind.

I'm not doom and gloom when I come home.

I'm focused on this incredible woman.

And that's why I'm never going to let her go.

"How's that champagne?" I ask, buying myself some time.

"Perfect."

Willow sips and takes in the setting sun. It's almost a mirror of how it was all those nights ago. You know when something is meant to be when all the stars fall into place so perfectly.

My hands begin to sweat. *It's time.* I have to do it before it gets dark. The ring won't gleam and shimmer in the darkness. It has to be now.

"Perfect… huh?" I scoot over so I'm directly beside Willow. "Much like you then…"

I wince at my cheesy words. Willow even frowns and glances sideways.

Just fucking get it over with, dickhead.

"Willow…" I grab the hand resting on her thigh. "Before we start this break together… There's something I wanted to ask you…"

Willow spins to face me, her eyes igniting. Panic pulls at her cheeks, and they begin to flush with a tiny hint of pink.

"Oh, this isn't about that thing we did last night, is it? I only did it because I read it in this steamy romance book and I wanted to try it… If you don't like it, I won't do it again. I promise."

I shake my head and laugh. "No. No. I liked *that.*"

Willow's face drops. "Oh. Then what is it, baby?"

The tiny waves in the river sound deafening. The sun is too bright. The non-existent wind is too strong. Fuck. Fuck. Fuck!

"Hello?" Willow waves a hand across my face.

"Right." I spin to face her, drawing in three long, deep breaths. "Willow. This past year has been both the best and the worst year of my life." I see Willow's face drop. Not the best start. "Hear me out. It's been the best, because I met you. Every minute that I'm with you it's like the world is a better place."

A tight smile. *Better*.

Willow sips her champagne and I'm starting to wish I'd had at least two glasses myself.

"It's been the worst year, because every time I have to leave you…" I choke on the lump in my throat. I feel tears forming in my eyes. I promised myself I wouldn't cry. I'm a Navy SEAL, dammit. "Every time I have to leave, a piece of me breaks inside."

Willow grips my hand.

"Willow, I love you. And I never want to leave you again."

A tear rolls down my cheek and Willow's eyes begin to swell.

"My time offshore is finished. And I want to celebrate." I reach in my pocket and pluck the tiny box out. Willow sees and instantly covers her mouth with a clenched fist. "I'm home forever, baby. And I want to marry you. Will you do me the honor of being my wife?"

Willow throws her arms around my neck, sending my champagne glass smashing to the grass.

"Yes! Oh my god, yes!"

"Really?" I burst up, tears free flowing down my cheeks.

"Of course! I'm getting married!"

Willow shoots to her feet and she's bouncing on her heels. I grab her hand and slide the ring on her finger, pulling her in and pressing a deep, sensual kiss to my fiancé.

"Are you really home forever?" Willow asks, unable to remove her gaze from the ring glistening in the sunset.

"Yes. I'm still continuing service, but I'm onshore from now on baby."

Willow steps forward and crawls a teasing finger across my chest. She leans up on her tiptoes and her lips tickle my earlobe.

"Does that mean we can start trying for a baby?"

"Now?" I spin and look around. "The tree still looks good. Plus, we have a picnic blanket this time."

Willow smiles. "Put a baby in me, mister."

"Affirmative."

THE END... FOR NOW.

This was Ryan and Willow's story. If you thought this was steamy, it's got nothing on Operation SEAL Her.
If you love strong military men and friends to lover's romance, I know you'll love Jack and Riley's story in Operation SEAL Her.
Keep reading for a peek at Book Two of the Operation Curves Series.

EXCERPT FROM NEXT IN SERIES...

Operation SEAL Her – Book Two

My best friend. My first true love. The problem is... I've never told her how I feel.

Operation SEAL Her – Book Two

Chapter One

Jack

I let the momentum of my body take me over the edge of the path and the wind howls across my face. The view is just as spectacular as I remember. Even through my strained exhausted expression I can make out the tiny, dotted buildings that make up the small town where I grew up.

The jog up the only rise of earth in Falls Creek is tough, even for a physically fit young man. So a Navy SEAL who undergoes intense training day-in-day-out should barely squeeze a drop of sweat up the incline, right?

Wrong.

And I'm not blaming the three beers I downed at lunch either. But the view. Oh, the view…

It's home. And it's damned good to be back.

I suck in deep breaths, circling the dry grass with my hands behind my head. My heart is pounding inside my chest. *Dammit. I need to stay fit.* I've only been on leave for a few days, but when it's your job to remain at peak physical condition at all times, it only takes a few bad meals and some cheeky lunchtime beers to knock your body around.

Searching for breath, I look around my old hang out spot. The same wooden seat is slightly more worn than I remember. A smile touches my lips. The memory of when I would sit up here, staring over the flowing river with my school buddies, drinking warm beer and smoking rolled up cigarettes like tomorrow was never going to come.

Those were the days.

It's a world apart from where I am now.

Jumping out of helicopters. Praying… Hoping that the chute will open when I yank on it. Not that it gets any safer when I float into the soft, evergreen floor of the dense rainforests in Southeast Asia. The second we touch down, you can bet your ass we'll be ambushed by armed civilians. Or gunshots aimed in our direction will have us crawling through the fallen leaves for our fucking lives.

I'm Jack 'The Rig' Brooks. I'm a US Navy SEAL.

Alongside my brothers, we make up one of the toughest units in the United States defense. We fight for freedom. We fight for our rights.

And goddammit, we fight for each other.

I sink down on the hard bench and pull on my toes, stretching my calves while admiring the view. It's always bittersweet coming home to Falls Creek. Everything about the place feels like home. The smells. The people. The house we live in.

I love it all. That's why I'm here.

Despite that, something always feels like it's missing. Falls Creek might *feel* like home, but is it really?

My parents retiring and moving across to Hawaii to soak in the warmth of the sun might have something to do with it. At the start of my career, they were the reason we would all come back here when we were granted leave. Now, the house we all grew up in is abandoned for most of the year.

I don't know what the pull of coming home to Falls Creek is, but I know that one day I'll find out.

The raging heat from the sun beams down on me. I'm sweating like I'm back in the depths of the dense tropical heat.

I'm sitting on the same bench I was fifteen years ago, only now, I'm not a drunk teenager. I'm a grown ass man who had two beers with lunch, and straight after this jog, I'm heading straight back to the bar to meet up with an old friend for some more.

So what? I'm on leave and I'll get damn drunk if I want to.

I take a quick glance at my phone and my eyes pop. I'm due to meet an old buddy shortly and I still need to jog down this bitch of a hill. Lucky, the jog down is much easier than the struggle up here.

I go to push up from the bench, and as I do, I notice a scratching in the timber of the old bench seat. It's scattered with graffiti, etched into the grain of the wood like ancient hieroglyphics. One engraving in particular catches my eye and my thumb traces over the letters.

Jack + RileyAlways and Forever

My heart beats fast from a combination of fear and excitement. A nervous twist pulls inside my chest and I force myself to my feet. Ignoring the fleeting feeling in my belly, I brush myself down and focus. I run away from the bench and despite all my efforts, the memories of days gone by race across my mind.

It was a long time ago. Why can I still see her smile? The tiny rays of sunshine that lit up my life like no other… They're still there. They're always there.

It doesn't matter, I tell myself. *She never looked at you like that.*

My pace is fast down the hill. My arms pump like I'm running through the dusty streets of the Middle East again. My brothers and me have been taken all around the world, and flashbacks of previous missions are often hard to force to the back of my mind. Just ask my brother Ryan, he's struggled with PTSD for years. Poor bastard.

We all look out for each other, though, and when I sprint inside our home, I throw a quick wave to Benjamin, the oldest of us four brothers. The scratching in the bench seat has me rattled and I need a cold shower to get my mind straight before a big night out with some old mates from high school.

"We'll always be friends, you know? Always."

"Forever?"

"Forever."

My old buddy will be waiting at the local bar, *Stagger and Slur.* He's the kind of guy you don't want to keep waiting. Even if you are a big, burly Navy guy. So I give my wet hair a quick toweling and toss on the first pair of jeans I can find. A white tee-shirt will do tonight. Even when the sun sets in the distance, Falls Creek encompasses the sweltering heat late into the night.

I race down the stairs and overhear Benjamin telling Maverick about some girl next door. Maverick is only a year older than me. He's shy and withdrawn, so why Benjamin is bothering to encourage him to get out of the house, I have no idea.

I slam the door shut and pace down the streets towards the bar. My mouth is watering already, and the smell of deep-fried jalapeño-poppers and arancini balls has my tastebuds alive before I'm even sitting at the bar.

I scan the place. It's habit. Ever since I've undergone specialized training in California. *Be aware of your surroundings at all times.* The jukebox in the corner looks broken. The display is smashed and the neon lights are no longer glowing in the dark corner of the room. The eight-ball table is new – the one I used to play on had red felt – not blue.

I pull the barstool out and continue looking around, allowing a tight smile to lift my lips.

"I was starting to think you weren't going to show up." A voice from behind me forces me to spin around quickly, and when my eyes focus on the giant man in front of me, I burst from my seat.

"Gabe! You big mother fucker!"

A giant hand slaps me on the back. Gabriel is a professional hockey player, and fuck me, he's been hitting the gym hard this season.

"Will you ever stop beefing out, man?"

My eyes gawk at the sheer size of the man. I'm not exactly small, standing in at six foot six. But next to this hulking, thick stout of a man, I feel puny.

"I thought the military would be pumping you with shit to get your tiny ass at a decent size," Gabriel says, his voice deep.

"Fuck off, man," I grin.

I observe him for a moment and see a fresh scratch on his forearm. He notices my gaze and rolls a large hand over the graze. "Hockey injury. Don't worry – I chased him down."

I've heard about the antics of the new Falls Creek hockey team. A collection of bad boy assholes who own the ice they skate on – whether it belongs to them or not.

And standing opposite Gabriel, I'm rethinking the hurried message I sent him demanding a catch up tonight.

"I bet you chased him down, man…" I smile and shuffle back on the barstool. "Sit down. What's been going on?"

I slide another stool out and Gabriel starts telling me all about life in Falls Creek. The barman pulls the draft tap and slides a few lagers down. We clink our glasses to the reunion. Gabe tells me about how he moved away for a while, but similar to me and my brothers, he's back. It's home and the attraction of this sleepy, tiny town has claimed another victim. A giant fucking victim at that.

"So, anyway… We're hitting the league hard, and I think we're in for a shot at the playoffs."

"Shit man, that's awesome."

"Not as awesome as what you're doing… Fucking four Navy SEALs in one town? One family?!" Gabriel's eyes pop. I'm used to the shock, though. The Brooks family is famous even within the platoons back in California. "Have you been doing some cool stuff? Swiping terrorists off the face of the earth?"

"I can't really say…" I sip my beer and avoid Gabriel's intense gaze.

"Nothing? Not a word."

I shake my head, my lips tightly sealed.

Time passes by quickly. We're chatting like the old days, and I know I'm going to regret the three empty glasses in front of me when I try to jog up that fucking hill again tomorrow. The bar has filled and the dark sky outside is bringing the crowd in. Guys and girls, all dressed to impress despite it being so early in the week. The pool table is stacked with young guys, all laughing and playing each other for money.

The girls are all looking fabulous. I catch Gabriel's eager eyes hovering over one particular curvy bombshell in the distance. He's hungry for her; I can see the lust in the way he's gripping his empty glass in those giant bear-like hands of his.

"They don't make them like that anywhere else," I say, gesturing to the girl Gabe's keeping a close, protective, eye on. "Falls Creek's finest."

"You can say that again." Gabe's top lip twitches when a guy steams across and tucks a strand of the girl's hair behind her ear.

Usually, Gabe and I would be on the floor, pursuing our lady of the night. At least, that's how it used to be. Me and the boys. Out on the town. Picking up the ladies. I've been known to 'play the field', but for some reason, tonight, I'm just not feeling it.

Jack + Riley. Jack + Riley. Jack + Riley.

The image rolls around in my head. Flashbacks of the girl sitting on my lap, smiling as she gripped my hand melt my insides. The memory is vivid – we used my old army knife to scratch the words in the seat, her hand clasped over mine as she giggled with every letter we drew.

I can hear the soft trill of her laughter. I can still feel her sweet, lusciously curvy figure in my lap as if it was yesterday. I can feel her warm breath teasing my neck.

A deep sigh leaves my chest.

Riley Stewart was my biggest crush.

She was also my best friend.

The problem is, I've never told her how I feel about her.

Get Operation Seal Her HERE!

Also By C.H. James

MORE BOOKS BY C.H. JAMES?

Want more? Yes, please!

Instalove Short Reads:

Curvy Girl Getaway Series

Broken Promise

Spanish Secret

Kiss at Midnight

Rebound Suite

Curvy Girl Getaway Series - The Complete Collection

Curvy Kilts Series

Andrew – My First Love

Robert – My Older Man

The Locker Room Series

My Curvy Puck

Captain's Curvy Puck

Puck My Roommate

My Virgin Puck

My Grumpy Puck
My Perfect Puck
The Locker Room Series - The Complete Collection

Operation: Curvy - A Navy SEAL Series
Sealing Her Fate
Operation SEAL Her
Surrender To Her
Her Curvy Explosion

Falls Creek Falcons – A Bad Boy Hockey Romance Series
Bad Boys: Shut Out
Bad Boys: Game Over
Bad Boys: Pressure
Bad Boys: Hard Play

Mountain Men of Falls Creek – A Steamy Mountain Man Romance Series
Curvy Cabin
Curvy Camper
Wet and Wild

Curvy Christmas Collection – A Plus Size Holiday Romance Series
Santa's Sack
Billionaire's Naughty Elf

Rough and Rugged – A Mountain Man Romance Series
Trapped by the Mountain Man

Club Zero – A Billionaire Romance Series
My Boyfriend's Billionaire Father
Single Mom's Billionaire Daddy
My Grumpy Billionaire Boss
Faking My Billionaire Husband

About the Author

STEAM. ALPHA. HEA.

INSTALOVE.

Bestselling author C.H. James writes short, spicy, addictive stories. Escape the real world in exotic locations with hot heroes
and relatable characters. There is ALWAYS a happily ever after,
leaving you satisfied and hungry for more.

A steady stream of new releases will keep you busy, so please
follow C.H. James by signing up to the newsletter at: https://b
it.ly/chjamesnewsletter

Ingram Content Group UK Ltd.
Milton Keynes UK
UKHW021946080523
421401UK00015B/1033